written by VARIAN JOHNSON
illustrated by SHANNON WRIGHT

An Imprint of
SCHOLASTIC

Library of Congress Control Number: 2019950320

ISBN 978-1-338-23617-0 (hardcover)
ISBN 978-1-338-23613-2 (paperback)

10 9 8 7 6 5 4 3 2 1   20 21 22 23 24

Printed in China 62
First edition, October 2020
Edited by Cassandra Pelham Fulton and Nick Thomas
Book design by Shivana Sookdeo
Creative Director: Phil Falco
Publisher: David Saylor

Sorry, girls, but this one is
for Brad and Andrea

V. J.

For my brothers, Duke and Travis, my
mentor, Kelly, and of course, Brandon

S. W.

CHAPTER 1
O'CONNOR
MIDDLE SCHOOL

Sixth grade! First day of the rest of your lives!

Remember, try new things! Make new friends!

It's okay if you're not the smartest --
Dad, this line is super long. Can you let us out here?

Sure thing.
What do you say, Maureen?

Maureen?

Um...
Sure. I guess.

Never mind. I'll drop you guys off up front.
But Dad...

Patience, Francine.

Dad, this line isn't even moving.

Do you really want us to be late on the first day of school?
Save your breath. We're staying in line.

TAP! TAP!

Hm...I'm going to be cutting it close for that meeting...

Sorry, Maureen...

Y'all better get out after all.
YESSS!!!

SMOOCH
KISS

Stop studying your schedule.
It won't be that bad.
You're not the one stuck in Cadet Corps and first lunch.

There'll be plenty of other kids who you know in first lunch.
Name three.

...Well, at least you don't have to take PE. I'll be sweaty before noon.
You saying you want to trade Cadet Corps for gym?

You know me. I look horrible in olive green.
UGH

Why are you so stressed? You're going to ace your classes. You always do.
Yeah, but --
But what? Come on, Maureen. Can't you **try** to pretend you want to be here?
There. Better. Any other problems?
Yeah, you missed a call this morning.
Who? Nikki?
The eighties. They want their hat back.

Hey, Amber! Be honest -- do you like my hat?
Dad had a saying for the two of us.

Throwback! Love it, Maureen!

I'm not --
Never mind. Thanks.

Francine was the talker, and I was the thinker.
You should have asked if she had first lunch.
There's no way I could sit with Amber! And **you** should have asked her.
Well, that's the way it used to be.

Something was happening with Francine. She was changing. Pulling away.
They're super smart! They graduated at the top of our fifth-grade class.
Are those the Carter twins?
It didn't hit me until she bought that ridiculous hat and T-shirt.

She wanted to make sure no one at school confused us.
Nice retro kicks, Maureen!
Though, thanks to a computer glitch, we only had advisory, science, and language arts together.

Whoa! Twins! I heard this joke about twins once...
She should have saved her money.

Francine and I are identical twins. There are, like, a thousand differences between us...not that anyone notices.
1/4-inch shorter
Slight overbite
Ragged fingernails
Scars from chicken pox (Mom said not to scratch!)
MAUREEN

FRANCINE
One pound heavier
Pierced ears
Two beauty marks
Small burn scar (Dad said not to play with matches!)

Of course, there'd be at least one day each week when we wouldn't look alike for sure.
Think you'll learn how to twirl one of those?
Maybe. I guess that would be kind of cool.
Wait, was I supposed to wear my uniform today?!
Maureen, you don't even **have** your uniform yet.
JAGUARS
Hey -- is that Bryce Jackson? He's a year ahead of us, right?
JACKSON
If that's him, he's gotten a lot... taller.
Who knew you could wear olive green and still look cute?
Bryce could wear anything and look cute.
Maybe you lucked up with getting Cadet Corps after --
Francine! Maureen! Over here!

??!!
??!!
I...I...

Hey, guys!
NIKKI
TASHA
MONIQUE

My sister told me how some kids want to act all funny in middle school.
Like they're too cool for their old friends. Not us!
No, you're right. Y'all do look cute.
I'm just surprised. That's all.
At least now I can ditch this silly hat. You're so lucky to be dressed different.
Francine would have beaten me to a pulp if I had tried to --
RING!
Gotta go. See you at -- oh, yeah. You're not in our lunch. I'll find you between classes!
Bye, Monique!

I can't believe those guys!
Sorry!
WATCH IT!

We're in middle school now. Only babies dress alike.
Babies. And twins.

Do you know where you're going?!
OUCH !!!

I think advisory is down this hall.

Francine, did you --

Francine?

RIIING!!
What happened to you?!
Sorry.
Guess we got separated.

Quiet down, students. I'm Mrs. Barbosa. Welcome to advisory!
Don't forget to ask about lunch.
Shh!

Savannah?
Here!
Marcus?
Present!
Sydney?
Here!

Francine?
Actually, it's Fran.

Does that make you **Maur?**
Maureen is fine, thank you.

Francine?
Are you going to ask about lunch?
Francine had promised last night to ask about the lunch periods.
Hmph. FINE.
I guess Fran conveniently forgot.
Mrs. Barbosa?
Yes, Fran?
Sorry, I'm Maureen... and I'm a little confused about when I'm supposed to eat lunch.
You report between fourth and fifth period.
Yes, ma'am. So that means I go to class first?

Of course you're supposed to go to class.
Okay, so I report to fifth period, **then** lunch.

You have lunch **between** fourth and fifth period. Young lady, are you trying to be smart?
No, ma'am! I just wasn't sure if I was supposed to go to fifth period and walk to the cafeteria with my class...

We don't hold hands to walk to the cafeteria. You go to lunch, then report to fifth period.

Thanks a lot!
Calm down. It's just lunch. How hard could it be?

I planned it all out during science class. I figured my best chance of eating lunch with someone I knew was to catch them before they entered the cafeteria.
WELCOME BACK
JAGUARS
FIND YOUR SPOT
I knew some of the kids...

WELCOME BACK
JAGUARS
TOO LOUD
TOO POPULAR
TOO MEAN
TOO DIVA

WON'T REMEMBER ME
WELCOME BACK
JAGUARS
FIND YOUR SPOT!
STUDENT COUNCIL? BE A LEADER! SIGN UP!!!
THROWS FOOD
In the end, no one seemed like a good fit.

SLAM!

inhale

LAND of Glitter
JOCK MOUNTAIN!
EIGHTH GRADE PASSAGE
EX

VALLEY OF BURPS & SMELLS
WET FLOOR
RIBBON RAVINE

It took a while, but eventually I found a seat.
Can I sit here?
Sorry, this is Gracie's seat.
But we can share! I can slide over and --
No! That's okay!
SWOOSH
At least there was one benefit of reading through all my orientation materials...

NO-MAN'S-LAND

After lunch

I am Master Sergeant Lucinda Fields.
Your instructor for the Youth Cadet Corps program.
At least I knew some kids in Cadet Corps.

GULP
Prior to this, I served our great country as a member of the United States Army.

I did many tours abroad. Afghanistan. Korea.

CADET! GIVE ME TEN!
AHHHHH!!!...

Dollars?
Address me as Master Sergeant or ma'am. And I'm talking about push-ups, Cadet.
Now get to it before I add ten more.

Those of you new to YCC will begin as cadets.
There will be opportunities to earn rank throughout the year.
One...two...three...

Your class leader is Private First Class Bryce Jackson.
Private, come up and brief the cadets on our procedures.
Eight...nine...ten!!!

Good job, Garcia. Go ahead and take a seat.

??

After explaining the classroom procedures, Bryce -- er, Private Jackson -- led us to the parking lot to practice marching.
SQUAD, ATTEN-HUT!
Some positions were really easy.
LEFT FACE!
RIGHT FACE!
ABOUT FACE!
OOF!
Others...not so much.

Good job! Tomorrow we'll try **real** marching!
SQUAD, DISMISSED!
PANT
HUFF

That was fun!
You **like** marching?

Better than running around the gym all year.

Hey, sorry we didn't have room for you at lunch. Where'd you end up sitting?
I, um, found a quiet spot.

Oh, good.
GULP!

I was worried that you ended up by yourself in the library or something.
SPIT!
Talk about depressing!

My legs were still sore when I got home.
...But by far, my favorite class was chorus.
I fall between soprano and alto. Ms. Ryan put me with altos for now.
And I think I'm going to run for student council.
Maybe even pres --
I want to hear all about it, honey. But let's give Maureen a chance to talk about her day, okay?

My day was fine.
I liked coding class.

What about Cadet Corps? They promote you to captain yet?
It was... sweaty.
But speaking of that...

In math, Julia told me she was switching PE for Cadet Corps, so I thought, maybe I could take **her** spot in PE.

It's the same time Francine has PE. We'd be in another class together!

I think you should give Cadet Corps a shot. You might really like it.

At least you get to march with Bryce Jack --
Shut up, Francine!
My bad. I mean **FRAN.**

Wait, you're going by a different name?
I wanted to try something new.

Francine was your great-grandmother's name --
Who was born, like, a hundred years ago. Francine hasn't been a cool name since.

Nothing wrong with trying out a new name, honey. I mean, **Fran.**
She was born ninety-five years ago...
I'm not changing **my** name, Dad.
Well I heard you ate lunch in the library. Were you too scared --
I-I was working on a project!
Mom, will you tell Francine to stop spying on me?!
Will you tell her to call me Fran?!
Excuse me for trying to name you girls something unique.

CHAPTER 2
SISTERS
M
6:29

RING!
RING!
RING!
6:30

~~Ugh
CLICK

Too bright!
You can't hide in bed forever.

Should I wear the red or blue?

Maureen?

Quit faking.
You're usually up before I am.

I can't believe you're excited about going back.
It wasn't that bad, was it?

How did you know I was in the library yesterday?
Ronnie told me. He saw you running out of the cafeteria.

I wasn't running!
It was a brisk walk.

I was just checking up on you. That's what older sisters do.
Two minutes isn't older.
PLOP

It's just... everything is different. Harder. But everyone seems to be doing fine. Except me.
Yesterday wasn't great for me, either. My voice cracked three times in chorus. Bobby and his friends laughed.
Bobby's horrible.
It's like every other kid has either taken private lessons or is a natural-born singer.
You just need to practice. And wear the red.
Things will get better for us both. Try sitting with some of the Cadet Corps kids at lunch.
Like, I don't know...someone whose name begins with B and ends with ICCCCE??

Francine was right about some things. Science class was a lot better on Tuesday.
We form a hypothesis!
Correct!

And language arts was better on Wednesday.
Watch out, Maya Angelou! Here comes Maureen Carter!

I even found ways to see my friends between classes.

I'm going to the mall with Nikki and Tasha after school. Wanna come?
I'll check with Francine.

Okay! Don't leave me hanging!

But Francine wasn't right about everything.

SWING!
She was always the more popular one. The talkative one.
She could make friends with a rock.
She had even decided to run for class president, and was forming a campaign committee and everything.
You're not supposed to eat in the library, but Mrs. Colbert hasn't said anything yet. She always smiles at me -- I think she likes me.
Or maybe she just thinks I'm Francine.

After school
Where is she?
HONK!
Maureen! Over here!
Curtis!
Curtis is our older brother. Well, technically he's our half brother, but we never think of him like that.
Curtis lived with us during college, but moved out this summer after Dad helped him find an apartment as a graduation present.
Dad's tied up and Diane's still at work, so I offered to pick you up.
Thanks! Want me to hunt down Francine?

It's just me and you. Francine's got some after-school thing.
She didn't mention that this morning. Or in class.

So...how's life as a first-grade teacher?

No kid has thrown up on me yet. Then again, it's only Wednesday.

Forget about me, how are you doing?
Um, have you talked to Francine?

No. Why?
Then it's going great!
Maureen...
It's just... hard.
Hang in there. It'll get better.
That's what everyone keeps saying.
Anything I can do to cheer you up?
Actually, yeah. Can I borrow your phone?

Loopde SCOOP!
MAM
SLICE
GYR
NOW

BUUZZ!!
It's Nikki.
I'm telling her where we are.
When did she get a phone?
This summer.
Y'all are growing up so fast! Want me to give you Dad's rules about walking around the mall?
I'll take NO for a thousand, Alex.

I'm telling you -- it seems like yesterday that I was changing your diaper.
Did you used to walk ten miles to school, uphill, barefoot, in the snow, too?
Ha ha. It was actually --
There they are!
Just remember, the mall can be a dangerous place!
We're leaving, Curtis!
Okay. I'll be right here if you need me!

My mom tried to give me a big speech, too! We're not babies!

NOD
NOD
NOD
I know! We can walk around the mall by ourselves!

You saved Curtis's number in your phone, right?
NOD

Hey. No Fran?
TAP TAP
I don't know where **Francine** is. She had other plans.

Too bad for her. She missed out on a free ice cream --
Quiet! They're coming!

Hey, girls!
See you tomorrow!

Geoff is so cute!
Yuck! He looks like a turtle! But did you see how Javier smiled at me?
Eighth graders. They're in after-school jazz band together.

There were worse ways to spend an hour. It almost felt...I don't know... normal.
TEMPORARILY 22
SALE!!
Except for the fact that we were down a girl.

I had known Nikki and Tasha since kindergarten. We all played together, but I wouldn't have called us best friends or anything.
Then Monique showed up in third grade.
Before I knew it, we were inseparable.

Dad called Monique the fifth gear. The one who made our "friendship-mobile" run smoothly.

FRANCINE

TASHA

MAUREEN

MONIQUE

NIKKI

POOF!

TASHA

MAUREEN

MONIQUE

NIKKI

But would our friendship still work if we were missing a piece?

Y'all go ahead.
We'll wait here.

You can stop with all the pretend smiling, Maureen.
I'm not --
You don't wanna be here any more than I do. At least I can fake it better than you.

So why come if you don't want to be here?
Now that Angela's in college, the house is too quiet.

And if I have to pick between being bored at home or walking around the mall...

Well, I pick the mall.
I guess...

Francine was home by the time I got there.
Hey, where were you after school?
I had a chorus thing.
Why didn't you tell me? I could have waited.
You would have been bored.
Mom said you went to the mall.
Yeah. It was fun.

• • •

Well, it was **kind of** fun.
If I have to pick between being bored at home or walking around the mall, I pick the mall.

I guess.

Or maybe you just need more hobbies.

Speaking of other **hobbies...**
You are the sorriest bunch of cadets I have ever seen. You can't walk without tripping over your own two feet.
We will march three times a week until you get it right. If that doesn't work, we'll try five days.
Tomorrow is uniform day. Come by after school to pick up your clothes if you don't already have them.
Those shoes better be so shiny that I can see my reflection, Cadet.
Release the cadets, Jackson.
SQUAD, ATTEN-HUT! DIS-MISSED!

She hates us.
You're exaggerating.

Fine. She hates **me.**

Come on! Can't you lie to make me feel better?
HA HA HA
HA HA

Our creed says we're not supposed to lie.
Somebody's been reading their manual.

She's just giving you a hard time, Garcia. She doesn't hate anyone.
Well, except Nazis.
Was she joking about drill five days a week?

Afraid not. It's important. Drill is twenty percent of our grade.

Don't worry, though!
Master Sergeant Fields has never failed anyone for not being able to march!

Cadet Carter. Do you have a second?

She hasn't failed anyone for being bad at drill, but it could drop you from an A to a B.
Or worse.

But Master Sergeant also gives you ways to earn extra credit! Ask her about it.
A-ask her?
Am I that bad? It's only the first week of school.
Well, like you said...
A cadet never lies!

After school
Uniforms are on the back rack, Cadet Carter.
Yes, sir. I mean, yes, ma'am. I mean, I know. I picked it up yesterday.
I stopped by because...well, I wanted --
Spit it out, Cadet. I don't get paid to read minds.
Bryce -- um, Private Jackson said you sometimes give extra credit.
So he told you that you were horrible at drill, huh? Good for him. Takes guts to tell a person they stink at something.
Cadet, what is the YCC mission?

Um -- to prepare
students to be
leaders...

SIGH

...With a commitment
to discipline, self-
confidence, integrity,
and...betterment of
self and community.

I see why you graduated
number one in elementary
school.
clap
clap
I did?

I could assign you
twenty extra-credit
essays and I bet
you'd ace each
one.
But that wouldn't
help you fulfill
our mission,
right?
I thought they didn't
track our rank...

From what I can tell, you have buckets of integrity and discipline, and you seem to be a positive influence on others.
But you are sorely lacking in self-confidence.
SEPTEMBER
And an essay won't do anything to improve that.
When your parents inquired about YCC, I promised I'd do everything I could to boost your self-confidence.
You talked to my parents?

Student council applications are due tomorrow. I'll give you extra credit if you run. Even more if you win.
They inquired about Cadet Corps?

What do you say?

Yes, ma'am. Thank you, Master Sergeant.

Um, Master Sergeant... what do you mean my parents **inquired** about YCC?

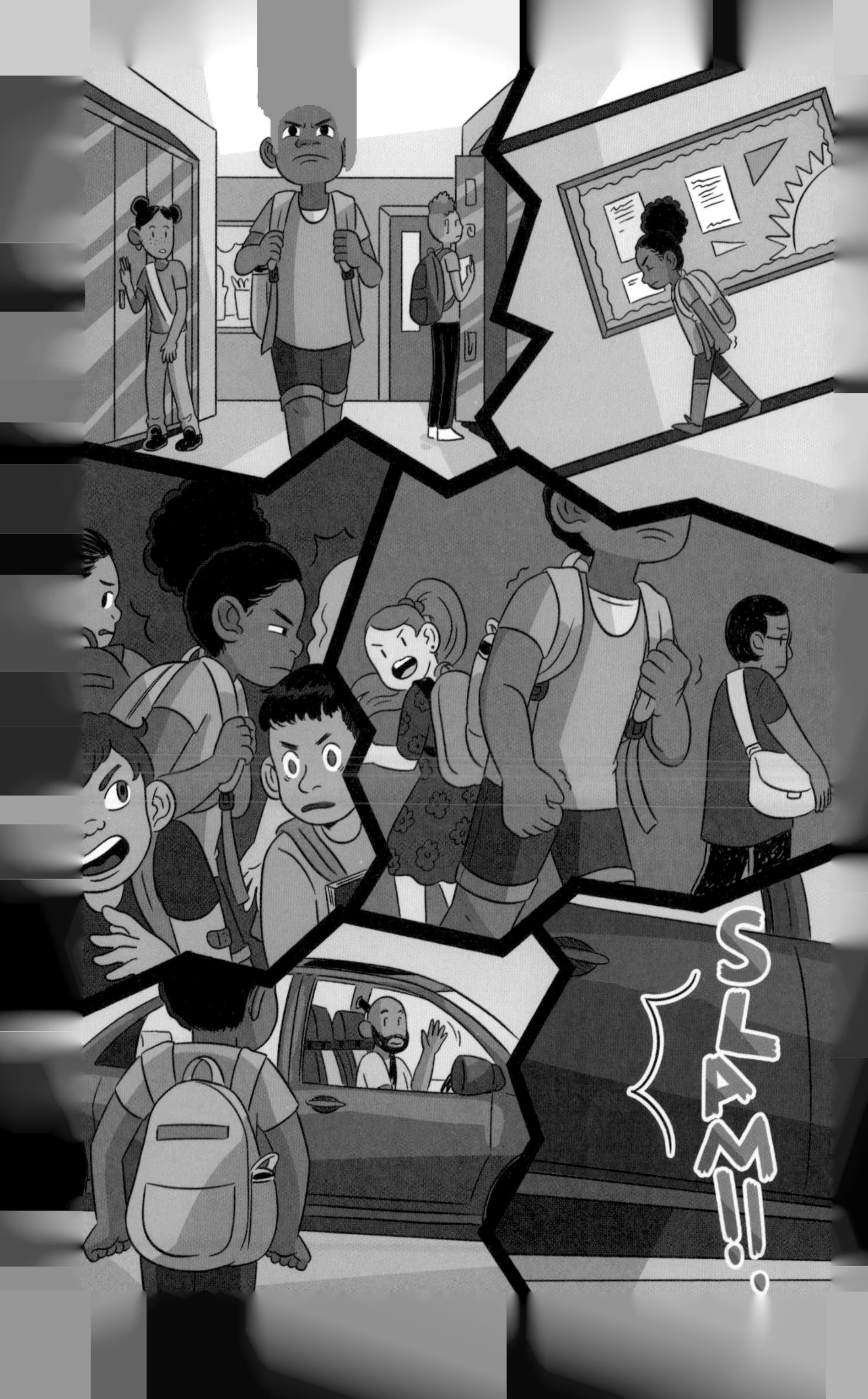
SLAM!!

Careful with the door, Maureen. Don't want to hurt the car's feelings.
Any idea where your sister is?

Oh, I remember! She's got a thing this afternoon.
Guess it's just us.

How long am I going to drive before you tell me what's wrong?

Hormones.

When were you going to tell me that you **ASKED** the school to put me in Cadet Corps?!?!

CHAPTER 3
SLAM!

We can talk about it if you really want more classes with your sister. Okay?

Maureen?

Harold, let's give her some time. We'll try again later.

POOF!
CREEEAK!!
I said to leave me --
FRANCINE!!!
Where were you?!
Did you talk to Mom and Dad?!
Did they tell you?!
Whoa. Can't breathe...

Sorry. Anyway, it **wasn't** a computer fluke that gave us different schedules.

Mom and Dad **asked** the school to do it!

And they stuck me in Cadet Corps because they don't think I have high self-confidence!
1
Can you believe it?!

But we can fix our schedules. You should probably switch to my Spanish and social studies classes.

I already have a partner for our class project, but I'm sure Penelope will understand if --
Maureen...

I don't want to change my schedule.

Fine. I guess I'll switch my classes. I don't like singing in public, but --
You don't get it.

I don't want **either** of us to change classes.
I **knew** it wasn't a computer glitch that caused our schedules to be different.
I asked Mom and Dad to put us in separate classes.

Aren't you tired of being THE CARTER TWINS? Don't you want to be your own person?
What? Why --
I know who I am. I don't care if people get us confused. Why should you?
It's not that we just look alike. Everyone thinks we're interchangeable. Like it doesn't matter if it's you or me.
That's easy for you to say. You're not the one stuck in Cadet Corps.
No offense, but you could use Cadet Corps. You **don't** have high self-confidence.

If you're so self-confident, why are you still hiding in the library during lunch?

M
4:42

Sleep on it. You'll feel better in the morning.

And tomorrow, maybe I can run some ideas for my campaign by you. I could use your help.

I, um...I was thinking about running for student council. But I guess you don't want me to...

No! It's not that I don't want to do anything with you. Just not **everything.**

What position? Treasurer, since you're so good at math? That'll boost your self-confidence for sure.

We can help each other with our platforms!

You'll have to give a speech in front of the school.
I know you hate public speaking.

Like I said, I was sick the morning of that speech.

Sure, sure...but still, you haven't tried to talk to a big group since then.

Don't worry -- I'll help you.

That's what big sisters are for, right?

The next day
Wow!
Looking sharp, Cadet!

Thanks.

So, about yesterday...

Francine and I talked. We're keeping separate schedules.

That's great!
You're giving it a try!

Thanks again for understanding. You're the best sister a girl could ask for.

I'm late for a meeting!
Be sure to put in your application for treasurer!

Ugh.

Cadet Carter!

Hey, Bryce. I mean -- Private First Class Jackson.

cough
cough

Oops!

And you can just address me as Private Jackson, Cadet.

The uniform looks good on you!
Makes you look taller! Sharper!

See you in class!

Excuse me. I'm interested in running for student council.
JAGUARS
Just fill this out and drop it in the basket when you're done.
PRESIDENT
VICE PRESIDENT
SECRETARY
TREASURER
HISTORIAN
scribble
Scribble
Scribble

6th GRADE
O'CONNOR MIDDLE SCHOOL
NAME: Maureen Carter
ADVISORY TEACHER: Mrs. Barbosa
POSITION RUNNING FOR:
PRESIDENT
VICE PRESIDENT
SECRETARY
TREASURER

CHAPTER 4

I planned to tell Francine about class elections first thing Saturday morning.
Then she ditched me to hang with her chorus friends.
10:03 AM
10:27 AM
10:56 AM
Eventually I called around to see what everyone was up to. Monique wasn't home, so I called Nikki.
I'd caught them as they were heading to the mall.
It was nice being with people who actually **wanted** to spend time with me.

SALE

SALE

Where are all the boys?!?!

SALE

Well, you did ask for boys...
Fine. Let's go shopping.
SALE

Come on, Nikki.
I mean, it's not like you actually want to **talk** to them.

Mercy DANGER

This is pretty! But I need a different size.

Must be nice to have a big allowance.

We were wondering if you had this --

I'll help you in a second.

I'm sure they'll wait. Probably just window-shopping or something.

Probably? That girl was trying to ask you a question and you ignored her. Why?
I'm sorry. It's just that, typically, you know --
Typically? What do you mean **typically?**

I'm getting the sudden urge to spend my money elsewhere.
Girls, I suggest you do the same.

!!!
TURN

Wait, I...
!!

!

If you think you can treat my girls any old way!

You have no right!!

I need to speak to a manager!!!

I told Mom what happened once I got home.

S%#&%!!!
She was a bit more colorful than Nikki's mom.

It was safe to say that we weren't ever shopping at Mercy Danger again.

I planned to tell Francine about it that night. About that... and the election.

Maureen? You awake?
But I was already asleep by the time she got home.

On Sunday, I promised God that I was going to tell Francine soon. Like after church.

Though, technically, I didn't say **immediately** after church.

After the service, we went to my favorite restaurant, the Wonderful World of Waffles.

And who wants to talk about election stuff while eating waffles?

At home, Curtis gave us a new game.

Francine even let me have first dibs.

I still want to talk to you about my platform. Have you thought about yours?

Um, I've got a few ideas.

I knew I had to tell her Monday morning.

But maybe when she was by herself. I didn't want to make a scene.

That left advisory.

There's something you should --
Teachers, please send all sixth-grade students running for student council to the library.

Time to meet the competition.
HEHEHE
GULP

Hello! I'm Mr. Wilson, your adviser for sixth-grade student council.

Fran
Carter...
And Maureen
Carter!
This is a first for
O'Connor Middle
School.
Twin
against
twin!

May the best woman win!

Francine!
Just wait a minute!

AH!
OOF!

I'm sorry, but I --
Maureen! I heard you and Fran were running against each other. That's kind of hard-core!

Um, you are Maureen, right?

Yeah, I'm Maureen.
And I guess I'm running for president.

What's your platform? Who's on your campaign committee?
I haven't really thought that far...

Well, count me in! I'm too chicken to run, but I have plenty of ideas!
You, chicken?

I also get extra credit in social studies if I help with a campaign.

Want to talk about it at lunch? We'll save you a seat at our table!
Okay?

Hey! Maureen!
Looking for Amber? Our table's by the wall.
You sit with Amber? I thought you sat with the boys.
I only hung with them on the first day because I didn't know anyone else.
Where do you usually sit?
Um...

I think it's awesome that you're running. I'm happy to help with posters or anything else.
What -- you're getting extra credit, too?
No! I just like helping my friends.
We're... friends???
Cool!

HA HA HA
*chomp
*chomp
HA HA

Francine didn't speak to me that afternoon, either.

She'd have to talk to me eventually.

SLAM!
I just didn't know what she would say.

You guys love slamming doors, don't you?
How was school?

So your Mom and I talked...

And since you guys have been so mature, especially about the schedule thing...

We decided to give you cell phones! Isn't that great?!

So, what do you think?

Maureen is ruining my life!
Francine won't talk to me!

CHAPTER 5

Now, what happened?
I chose to run for president. She copied me!
You told me I should run for an office!
NOT PRESIDENT!!! What type of sister runs against her own flesh and blood?!
What type of sister tells her other sister she doesn't have the self-confidence to --
I didn't say you had no self-confidence.
I said **low** self-confidence.
You stinking --
SLAM!
Both of you -- quiet down!!
Maureen, I have to ask -- do you really want to run for president?

I don't know. Maybe. Not really.
Well?
Of course I do! Plus, I need the extra credit.
YOU'RE ONLY RUNNING TO GET EXTRA POINTS IN CLASS?!?!
Tha-that's not the only reason!

But why president, Maureen? Fran has been talking about running since school began.
It feels disingenuous not to be honest about your intentions.

Oh, you mean disingenuous like how y'all put us in separate classes.
And then LIED about it?

Well, we **did** get you a cell phone...

So then are you only running because you're mad?
No. I have good ideas. I'm a leader -- whether you think so or not. I have a campaign committee and everything.

Quit if you don't want to run against me. Or what -- are you scared of a little competition?

Me? Scared?
Well, it **could** be good...
For both of them...

Okay. Clearly you both have the right to run. I don't like it...but we won't force either of you to drop out.
As long as you keep it civil.

No arguing at school. No smear campaigns.
If we find out you two are acting like anything other than sisters, you'll lose a lot more than those cell phones.

Mom and Dad sent us to our rooms so we could "make up" before dinner.

Why didn't you tell me?
FLOP!

I tried. But I didn't know how.
Plus, I was mad when you said I had no self-confidence. Or low. Whatever.

I know I was being mean when you said you wanted to change schedules.
I just...I'm tired of competing against you.
SIGH

What are you talking about? We don't compete against each other. I mean, other than in video games.

That's easy for you to say.
I don't understand what --
Forget it.

I need to call my campaign committee.

Hey, Monique! Ready to talk?
Good! But hold on...

Do you mind?
Do I mind **what?**

I'm on the phone.
And?

Can you leave? I don't want you to overhear my strategy.
Why can't you leave?

Besides, I don't want to hear your stupid ideas anyway!
My ideas aren't stupid!

And how come you get to have Monique on your committee?
TURN
Don't be mad because she chose the winning team!

Francine! That's not FAIR!
You want to talk about FAIR?!
Hello?
YOU LIED TO ME ABOUT RUNNING FOR PRESIDENT!!!
YOU LIED TO ME FIRST!!!

WHY IS EVERYONE YELLING?!?!
SLAM!

SHE STARTED IT!
Um, I'll call back...

Mom and Dad's idea of fairness was for both of us to leave the room for a while. I went to the living room.
Francine made her call from Curtis's old room.
I guess she really wanted privacy. I'd seen sewer grates cleaner than his room.
At dinner, Mom and Dad explained the new plan.
For the next two weeks, until the election was over, we would live in separate rooms.

One of us would stay in our room.
The other would take Curtis's room.
Dad made us flip for it.
FLIP!!!
SNATCH!
SLAPP!
Guess who lost.

I'll move the rest of my clothes tomorrow.
You don't have to move **everything.**

What about these? You can keep them for now. I'll take them next week.

Stop acting like we're getting divorced. You can come back to the room anytime you want.
You mean, except when you're on the phone. Or when you want your space.

You're not going to guilt me into feeling sorry for you.
Hm. I thought leaders were supposed to be compassionate.

It's just a stupid room! Why are you making such a big deal about everything?!
Because everything **IS** a big deal! We've never even slept ap--

I didn't have to finish. She knew what I was going to say.
Francine and I had never slept apart before.
We'd always shared a room. At camp. At our grandparents' house...

Even on that road trip where we shared a bed at every stop and Francine kept kneeing me in my back.
I could have slept with Grandma, but didn't.

Six years ago
Dad decided to stop at one of those roadside amusement parks on our way to Florida.
We didn't want to go on the rides or eat any food.
We only wanted the bears.

The way Dad tells it...

ERRR!!!

The game was rigged.

It took a while, but Dad eventually figured out how to win.

We named them Venus and Serena.

Since then, they'd traveled everywhere with us.
1
Thinking about taking Serena?

No, I think they'll be lonely without each other.

Wait! One last thing...

Whatever you do, **don't** open Curtis's top drawer.

KEEP
PUSHI

SLAM!!

SWOOP!

CLICK!

OAKWOOD COLLEGE
GO!

Do, re, mi, fa --
YAAAWWN~

Gotta run. Bye!

Then Mr. Harvey marched up to him...

HA HA HA

HA HA HA

Maureen!

Hey! You'll never guess what happened last night! I had to sleep in --
I'm sorry...
I'm actually looking for Fran. Know where she is? We're supposed to be talking strategy this morning.
She ran inside.
Thanks. Let's catch up tonight. Okay?
Yeah. Sure.

LET'S TALK STRATEGY!

Amber convinced me to wait until lunch for our meeting -- after I'd calmed down.

I heard you were running for class president. Good luck!
We're working on campaign ideas. Any suggestions?

No, but I'll let you know if I think of something.

While I'm here...study up on chapter one of your handbook. Master Sergeant always puts military history on the first exam.
Just something I wish I'd known as a first-year cadet.

That was nice of him to say.
He wasn't **that** nice. It's just his job.
Right, Maureen?

Maureen...?

Bryce! Got a second?

What else do you wish you knew when you were a sixth grader?
Not just cadet stuff. Everything.

Well, lunch on the first day was pretty confusing.
EXACTLY!

And I didn't know we were supposed to dress up for the October dance.
There's a dance in October?

I can probably make a list --
Is the seventh-grade president nice? Like you? Or are you only nice because you have to be?

I'm not nice because I have to be. I like being nice to you...
To all of you, I mean...

And just like that, I had a platform.

CHAPTER 6

6th Grade/7th Grade
BUDDY SYSTEM
CAMPAIGN
☆ TOTALLY VOLUNTARY PROGRAM ☆

- ~~Girls only w/ girls, boy with boys~~
  ↳ DUH! Gender is a construct
- Need to see if teams can meet during Advisory
- Work with ~~7th graders~~ all ages to develop FAQs
- How do kids sign up? Form?
- 8th graders? New students?
- System to keep it going!

Once we had the nuts and bolts of the platform, it was time to make posters.

Mom, this is Amber and Richard.
Hello! Nice to meet you kids!

I didn't realize you invited **new** friends over! That's great! But what about Nikki and Tasha?

They're staying out of the race. They don't want to choose sides. Not like Monique.
Be nice...

Do you mind working in your bedroom? Rachel is stopping by and I don't want to bore you with our conversation.
Ooh! That means y'all are talking about something juicy!

Hush!

To be clear, I meant **your** bedroom. Curtis's isn't suited for the general public.

But what about Francine? When she gets back...

She's with Curtis. I'll tell him to keep her for a little longer.

Can you hand me one of the big spoons?

What's she doing with Curtis?

I hadn't even thought about it -- a **boy** being in my room.

SMILE

MZA

SARUTO

BSC

You guys are so cute!

WHAT?!?!

You and Francine. Y'all were such cute babies.

Is Richard nervous about being in my room?
And what if he is? Does that mean...?

Hey? You okay? You're spacing out.

Oh, I'm fine.
SCRATCH

I just wish I had someone I could talk to about this.

Any idea how Fran's campaign is going?
Not sure. We haven't really discussed it.

It must be weird running against your sister.
Twin sister.
Yeah. Double weird.

What if you and Fran come up with the same platform?!
I don't think that'll happen.

But don't you guys share the same thoughts? You know, like twin psychic powers?

HAHAHAHA
HAHA
HAHA
It's not funny! I swear, I saw it on TV!

All joking aside, Richard does bring up a good point.

We need a way to make you stand out from Fran. Kids have to know they're voting for you, not her.

NOD
NOD
What about a photo?

Yeah, but not just any photo.

Nothing gets votes like a girl in uniform!

Loosen up. I've seen frozen fish sticks with more personality.

So what, you're a jellyfish now?

You're not even trying anymore!

CLICK!
Perfect!

We should use some of these photos as well.

What about this one?
BUZZZ!!!

BUZZ!
BUZZ!

Monique
Hey! Sorry for this morning
Got time to talk now?

Do you need to get that?
It's not important.

Okay. Well, take a look at this photo.
What do you think?
The school spelling bee isn't exactly presidential.
And maybe we shouldn't use a photo with Francine in it.
This one is pretty good!

The essay contest?

That photo makes me want to throw up. Literally.

You're being dramatic. We should take a vote.
Everyone who thinks we should use it, say aye.
SIGH

But --
AYE!!!

Done! The ayes have it!
SIGH

We didn't think it would be a problem to post photos of me in my uniform, but Amber made me check, just in case.

These look good, Cadet. I like how you squared your shoulders.

Also, exemplary job on your exam yesterday. It's evident that you studied.
Thank you, ma'am.

You'd be the perfect cadet -- if I could teach you how to march.

Master Sergeant, can I ask you a question?
You just did.
...Sorry, old joke. Go ahead.

Am I really that bad at drill, ma'am?

You're not the worst student I've ever seen... but you sure aren't the best.

Keep doing well on your tests, and you'll at least earn a B.
ugh...

Let me guess -- you've never received anything less than an A in a class.

No, ma'am. Not on a report card.

A B isn't the worst grade in the world, Cadet.

All I can say is -- **keep practicing!** Maybe we'll make a marcher out of you yet.
SLAP!!

I tried extra hard at drill practice that afternoon.

At least I didn't fall.
This time.

Hang in there. You really are getting better.

What's the point of running for president if I won't get enough extra credit for an A?

Is that the only reason you're running?

Not the only reason...
But aren't you serving on my campaign committee just for the extra credit?

Okay, yeah. I was at first. But now I'm doing it because I'm your friend.

Don't get me wrong, though -- the extra credit helps. Me and social studies don't mix.

Too bad we can't swap --
Maureen! Amber! You guys need to see this!

Giggle
HA HA HA!
GASP!

VOTE FOR MAUREEN!
BARF FACE!
GROSS
6th GRADE PREZ.
• Leader

Barf face!
Barf? That looks more like poop!
OMG, did she really throw up?
I'd die if someone drew something like that of me!

In fifth grade, I won a contest for Earth Day. My essay was chosen as the best paper in the entire district.
As an honor, I got to read it in front of the school.
Some honor.
I practiced for two weeks. Francine helped me. Every day.
But right before I was supposed to walk onstage...

DIVE

Lucky for me, I made it to the bathroom in time.

BLUURG!!
But I didn't make it to a stall.

sniff
Francine found me a few minutes later.
sniff
sniff
She tried to get me to go back onstage, but I couldn't.
So we came up with another plan.
I mean, we were identical twins. Who would know?

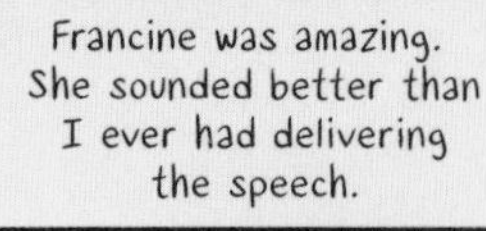
Francine was amazing.
She sounded better than
I ever had delivering
the speech.

She didn't even need to look at my
paper. She'd heard it so many times,
she had memorized it.

I never told any of my friends
what happened. I didn't tell a
teacher, either. Or our parents.
I was too embarrassed.
We promised to
keep it a secret.

Francine promised.

As soon as I saw Francine, I knew.
And she knew I knew.

Richard was right.

Sometimes we **could** read each other's minds.

I thought about confronting her then, but decided not to.

Curtis was coming over for dinner tonight.
I wanted them all to hear it at the same time.

CHAPTER 7

Maureen, Francine -- you two are pretty quiet. Don't like my cooking?
Like that's ever stopped them.

So... how's the election coming along?

Do you want to tell them, or should I?

I don't know what --
Don't. Just don't.
You promised -- no dirty politics.

Francine?

You had no right to use the photo! If it wasn't for me --

The me
was for w
the ess
not givin
speec

SLAM!

Okay, one of you needs to start explaining.

Now.

Francine vandalized one of my posters at school.

I promise, I didn't --
Stop lying! You drew vomit all over my poster. You called me Barf Face!

I'm not lying! I didn't draw it, I swear!

What are you two talking about? Throwing up? Vandalizing --
Hold on. Let them be.

Well, the last time I checked, you were the only person who knew what happened!

Do you know what they were saying? That if you're the smart one, the one with all the awards, then I must be the dumb one!

SWOOSH

You don't see me posting a photo of **my** medals.

No -- you were just telling all my secrets to your gym class!

It was an accident! I didn't mean to hurt you!

Well, you did!
YANK!
Look, if you hadn't run in the first place --

CLAP!
CLAP!

Enough!!!
We're going to try this again. From the beginning.
Without all the yelling.

Francine tried to explain, but they weren't having it.

Mom and Dad left to talk privately.
It didn't take them long to come to a decision.
Living room.
Now.

Francine, we are very, very disappointed in you. She is your sister.
You had no right to share her secret.
But --

Maureen, do you want Francine to report this to the school?
It may help them determine who actually vandalized your poster.

I just want to forget it ever happened.
And I don't want her to get into that much trouble.

That's very kind of you. But, Francine, that doesn't mean you're off the hook.
You're grounded indefinitely.

And, of course, you'll be dropping out of the election.
DAD!

Your mother and I aren't going to let you two tear each other apart over a silly election.
It's not silly.

You broke the rules, Francine. That has consequences.

With Francine out, I was guaranteed a win. No more posters or platforms. Maybe I wouldn't even have to give a speech.

That felt like cheating.

And most of the students wouldn't know I won. A vote for me would be like a vote for her. It would be like voting for the same person.

I don't want Francine to drop out.

at's nice of you, t you don't owe your sister nything in this matter.
And, quite frankly, it isn't your decision.

But if she doesn't run I'll never know...

I'll never know if I was good enough to win on my own.

Are you sure?
Yeah, I am.

Francine, do you have anything to say to your sister?
Thank you so much! I promise I won't do anything like that again.
I'll even take Curtis's room. You can move back into our room tonight.
Maureen's been sleeping in my room?!

If you really wanted to make it up to me...
If you really wanted to give me space...

You'd offer to move to Curtis's apartment.

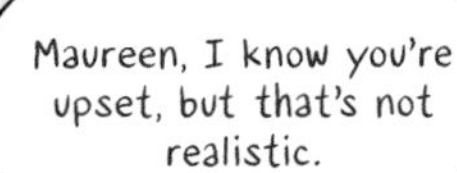
Maureen, I know you're upset, but that's not realistic.

Why not? Dad's always joking about moving us all out as soon as possible.

Um...your mother and I need to discuss --
scratch
scratch
I'll do it.

I caused all this mess. It's the least I can do.
That is, if it's okay with Curtis.

Um...sure? I guess that wouldn't be a problem. I mean --
ENOUGH!

I am not kicking one of my girls out of the house over this election!
But --

This is what we will do. Francine, you will do all your campaign work at Curtis's apartment or school.
Not a lick at home.

All election work for you both stops at dinnertime. We will eat together every night. As a family.
Understood?

NOD
NOD
Yes, ma'am.
NOD
NOD
Yes, Mom.

Curtis, does this work for you? Do you want to think it over?
It'll be okay, Diane. It really isn't any trouble.

scratch
scratch
But, um, when exactly is this election again?

After dinner, Francine went to pack up her election materials.
That was really nice, what you did for Francine.

It wasn't just for her.

Is school getting any better? Want to talk about it?
Things are good. I have a lot of friends.
Well, two -- Amber and Richard. And I guess Bryce is my friend, too.

What about Nikki, Tasha, and Monique?
SPLASH!!

Nikki and Tasha have been hanging with their band friends lately. And Monique is Francine's campaign manager, so...

Monique is still your friend.
BLOP!
And Francine is still your sister.

They have a funny way of showing it.

So...Richard and Bryce?
You sure they're **just** friends?

Duh! Of course they are!

Or, hey -- it's cool if you have a thing for Amber! Just don't go kissing anybody yet.
Plenty of time for that!

CURTIS! I don't want to kiss ANYONE!

I need to meet these friends of yours. Give them my stamp of approval.

You had your chance. They were here the other day when you dropped Francine off.

They were here? Where?
Don't worry, they weren't in your room.

SIGH

And even if they were, they would have never peeked in your top right dresser drawer.

But for real -- why didn't you tell me that you and Francine were hanging out? Y'all go to the mall?

It must have slipped my mind. I'll take you this weekend if you want to go. Just call and --

cough

Here's everything.
I guess I'll see you tomorrow?

Guys, I know things are difficult right now.

Just don't forget, y'all are sisters.

Bye, Dad! Bye, Diane! Thanks for dinner!

CLICK!

Need help with the dishes?
No, thanks. Almost done.

Are you sure? I can --
I'm good.

I know you don't believe me, but I promise, I'll find out who drew that picture on your poster.
I don't even care anymore.

And I'm still game for moving into Curtis's room.

Don't go doing me any favors. I'm fine where I am.

Maureen! Please! I just --
BUUZZ!!!

BUUUZZZ!!

Hey, Amber. Yeah, now's a good time to talk.

I wasn't doing anything important.

CHAPTER 8

Here's the funny thing about running for student council.

Most kids didn't really care about the election. Some would at least pretend to be interested.

Others, not so much.
BUDDY SYSTEM

But some kids did care.

And those kids seemed to really like my idea for a school buddy system.

Francine's platform was all about more interaction between clubs at school.

Like asking the chorus to sing while the orchestra accompanied them.

WANT YOUR CLUB TO BE SEEN? THEN VOTE 4 FRAN!

Or having the drama club perform skits at halftime during the basketball games.

She even suggested "Showcase Days" where clubs could perform during lunch.

Don't worry. Who wants to perform in front of a big group, anyway?

Oh, I don't know. Maybe the chorus. Or the band. Or the drama club...

Can't you do that program after you win? Your sister wouldn't mind, right?

Not sure, I'll have to ask her.
Once I start talking to her.

Don't take this the wrong way, but it would be kind of cool to do drill performances with a live band.
GRRR

What are traits of a good leader?

Communication?
Unlike me and Richard, Amber was acing Cadet Corps inside and outside the classroom.

Good job, Cadet. Any other --

Garcia, are you drawing again?!

You know the drill.
Though marching was the least of Richard's problems.

One...two...
Since I've been interrupted, I'll stop to remind you that I'm still looking to promote a cadet to squad leader.
Those of you who are interested --
I am, Master Sergeant!!
Three... four...
Can speak to me after class.
Fiiivvve...
I look forward to hearing from you. Well, most of you.
Siiiiiixxxx...
You haven't finished those push-ups yet?! My nana would be done by now, and she's dead!!

Amber offered to help me and Richard with drill after school. Plus, I'm sure she wanted to get some practice in for squad leader.

Why can't you just stop drawing in class?

Would you ask Picasso to stop drawing? Or Mozart to stop composing?

SHAKE

I would if their grades depended on it.

Maureen!

Glad I found you! I was wondering if --

Sorry, but we're heading to a campaign strategy meeting.

Oh. Okay.

I'll, um... catch you later, then...

Come on. We have plenty of campaign things to talk about after practice.

I wasn't really in the mood to march.

Cadet Garcia, is your spine made of mashed potatoes?

Square those shoulders, Cadet Carter.

SQUAD! RIGHT FACE!

Come on, Cadet! Stay focused!

Chill out, Amber. I know you want to be squad leader, but you don't have to act like a jerk.

You're the one who asked **me** for help!

I won't make that mistake again!

Fine. Walk off. Flunk! See if I care!!

If you can't tell, I really want to be squad leader.

And you'd be really good at it!

Thanks! Richard's afraid that I'll be mean to him if I'm in charge. But that's silly.

We'd be friends like before.
I mean, it's not like you and Fran will stop being sisters once you win the election.

She'd probably even be happy for you if you won. And you'd be happy for her. Right?

Yeah, I'd be happy.

Wouldn't I?

Bye, Curtis! See you tomorrow.

Curtis isn't coming in?
He's got plans with friends tonight.
Good. He can eat someone else out of house and home.

Go on and wash your hands. Food's about ready.

But I ate at --
Then eat again.

HeHeHe
Maureen, don't test your luck.

But how...?
Mom-sense. Works every time.

Tonight, your mother and I would like to hold a civil conversation about the election.

Fran, how is your campaign coming along?
Fine.

Why don't you tell us about it?
Consider it practice for your speech.

Wonderful! Great job keeping eye contact!

You had me from beginning to end!

Your turn, Maureen.
Picture us as your audience!

I wish he hadn't said that.

My platform is to form a...buddy system...

Where a sixth grader is paired with an, um, older kid. You know, probably a seventh grader.
HAHAHAHAHA

Or maybe an eighth grader? I, uh, haven't worked out those details yet...
Anyway, it's to help prepare us sixth graders for middle school...

That's a wonderful idea!
Awesome! You've got me hooked!

• • •

Yeah. Good platform, Maureen.

Can't you at least say it like you mean it?!

I do mean it! It's a good idea!
Everyone knows you always come up with the best ideas.

And it's not like you said **my** speech was good.
You've always been a good speaker!
Whatever.
SKRRT
Can I be excused?
Go ahead, sweetie.
So much for a civil conversation.

CHAPTER 9

For the next couple days, Francine and I did our best to steer clear of each other.

Dad said that things would return to normal once the election was over.

At least Amber and Richard weren't fighting anymore.

Richard even promised to "try harder" to pay attention.
SCRIBBLE
It helped that Amber began taking his sketchbook away before class.

And thanks to Amber's help, I was getting better at drill...
Good form, Cadet. You've been practicing.

OOF!
But maybe not good enough.

Hey, Maureen!
Are you looking for Francine? If so, she's --

Can we please stop. Okay?

Nikki and Tasha are coming over on Friday night.

I know things have been weird between us, but I want you to come, too.

Will **Fran** be there?

Funny.
Fran asked the same question about you.

Come on. I want it to be like before.

But everybody's different now! And not just Francine. Nikki and Tasha are always with their band friends.
And you --

Wait, what did I do?

You chose Francine's committee. You picked her over me.

Maureen...

Enough with the pity party!

It's not like you don't have other friends, too!
Yeah, but --

I didn't know you planned to run when I joined Fran's committee. None of us knew, remember?

I almost quit, but I didn't want to abandon Fran. Nikki and Tasha had already quit in order to be fair to you.

I didn't know they were on her committee in the first place.

Of course they were. We all were.
I wasn't! She never asked me!

You're sisters. She didn't think she **needed** to ask.

HONK!
I shouldn't say this... but ask Fran what she does when she's not working on election stuff.

Here's a hint--she's usually at school, but not hanging with friends.

I don't understand. You mean she's practicing with chorus?
Maureen!

Chorus is not an after-school activity.

HONK! HONK!
MONIQUE!
Coming, Mama!

I hope to
see you tomorrow.
Both of you!
But it's totally
cool if you come by
yourself! You're
your own person.
Just like
Fran!

CHORUS
VOTE
4
FRAN

2
x
7
TAP
TAP
9
10
11
12

Try another problem. But this time --

RING!

Was that a phone?
Must have been someone passing by. Let's get back to it.
MATH

Hey! Where were you?

I tried to call, but --
Master Sergeant Fields told me I graduated at the top of my fifth-grade class.

She did? Well, those are just unofficial rankings.

Put on your seat belt so --
Where did Francine rank?

It wasn't even a real graduation. And it's not really any of your --
Was she second? Third?

Why are you asking this?

Because I know Francine's getting tutored after school!

SIGH
When did you find out?
Just now.

I'm surprised we kept it a secret this long. What was she getting tutored in? Math? Social studies?

I didn't know there was more than one...

I won't say anything to her about it! Promise!
No. No more secrets.

Your mother and I should have never hidden all of this in the first place. That's what we get for trying to protect you two.
Sorry, Maureen. Our job is to make things better for you, not worse.

Fran was tenth.

Really? That's not bad!
Of course it's not! Your mother and I are very proud of Fran and the work she's doing.

Me too! And like you said, it's unofficial! It doesn't mean anything!

It means a lot when it's your twin who was ranked number one.

Put on your seat belt.
Let's go home.
O'CONNOR MIDDLE SCHOOL

If I really thought about it, there were plenty of times when Francine got upset about me being "smarter."
It's okay if you're not the smartest --
In the scientific method, what comes after performing research?
We form a conclusion?
Close, Fran. Maureen?
We form a hypothesis!
Watch out, Maya Angelou! Here comes Maureen Carter!
Good try, Fran, but this line works better...

Everyone knows you always come up with the best ideas.
We don't compete against each other. I mean, other than in video games...
That's easy for you to say.
But if I was being honest...

This had been going on for a lot longer than sixth grade.

Dad told me you found out.
Yeah. This afternoon.

I thought I recognized that ringtone.

PLOP!
Look, don't go making a big deal out of --
I'M SORRY FOR RUNNING FOR PRESIDENT!
Huh?!

I ran for the wrong reasons. I was mad.
And hurt.

PLOP!
It felt like you were throwing me away...

I should have told you about the class schedules.
But I was afraid that if I said anything, you'd convince me to change my mind.

I never meant to hurt you. I was mad, too.
Mad at how perfect you are.
I'm not perfect.
That's not what your grades say.
Wait 'til I get my Cadet Corps grade...
Why didn't you tell me that you had a tutor?
It's hard enough being the stupid twin. It's way worse admitting it to the world!
YOU'RE NOT STUPID!

Maureen, remember how Dad used to say that you were the thinker and I was the talker?

I wanted to be the thinker, too! I wanted to come up with good ideas, not just blab about them later.

But the worst was when everyone thought it was you who gave that speech for Earth Day.

There I was, finally good at something.

And they didn't even know it was me.

I'm sorry.
For everything.
Me too.

I'll drop out if you want me to.

Are you still running only to get back at me?
Not anymore. I like my platform!

It's a good idea!
Yours is, too!

We should both stay in. May the best woman win.
Sounds good... if you're okay calling me President Carter.
Maybe you'll be the one calling **me** president.
Just as long as I don't have to call you FRAN.
Oh, shut up...

For you, I'll always be Francine.

SISTERS
LOVE
5
EVA!

CHAPTER 10
DON'T STOP!

Francine and I decided not to go to Monique's house on Friday night.

Instead, we worked on our speeches.

We read them to our parents and Curtis on Saturday.

And on Sunday, we read them to our campaign committees.

Master Sergeant Fields, I know uniform day is usually on Friday, but I need a small favor...

You're going to do great!
Just remember to breathe.

If you get nervous, look for us.
We'll be right in the front --

Guys! Stop before you make me more nervous!

Sorry! Get up there and kick butt!

Sixth graders, thank you for your participation in the election process!
We'll start with our presidential candidates.
I was wrong, by the way.
First up -- Ms. Fran Carter!
We look great in olive green.

I remembered why Dad and I always called Francine "the talker."

She didn't even need notes.

She sounded like she should be in a church pulpit...
Not a school assembly.

And I wasn't the only one who felt that way.

Now let's welcome our second candidate -- Maureen Carter!
gulp
My turn.
Hello, my name is Maureen Carter...
Why did you say that?!
They know who you are. Mr. Wilson just said your name!
And I'm running for... for...
Don't tell them you're running for president, you idiot! They know that, too!
I'm...I'm...
Where are Amber and Richard?!
I'm here to tell you...to talk about...

PANT
PANT
Hey!
MAUREEN!
TAP
TAP

You got this.

I'm Maureen and I'm here to talk to you about the sixth-grade buddy system.
Because let's be honest. Everyone needs a buddy!
I don't even remember half of what I said, but the words felt right coming out of my mouth.

CLAP!
CLAP!
CLAP!
CLAP!
CLAP!
CLAP!
Maybe the words sounded right to them, too.

Things calmed down by the end of the day, and I almost forgot about the election.

Almost.

Maureen, Mr. Wilson would like to see you in his class.

Given the circumstances, I wanted to give you two the results before we announce them tomorrow morning.

Just in case things get emotional.

You should know, the votes were very close.

Closer than I've ever seen in a student council election.

But at the end of the day, there has to be a winner.

Maureen...

I'm sorry. You did not win the election.

It's okay if you want to cry.

It's totally understandable.

Maureen? Didn't you hear --
My sister lost?

But she worked so hard!

CHAPTER 11
Mercy
CLOSE OUT!!!
50%-80%
MUST GO!
STORE CLOSE OUT SALE
Everything Must Go!

Maureen!
I need to use the mirror!
It took a few weeks, but things eventually did return to normal.
I just got out of the shower! Can't you use the mirror in your room?!
I need more light!
Or, rather, the new normal.
Fine. Use my room. But don't touch my lip gloss.
I ended up staying in Curtis's room. Now it's all mine.

You know Dad's going to take a billion pictures.

I bet you five dollar
that he cries before
we leave.

Ten.

I HEARD
THAT!

Everyone *sniff* get together *sniff* for a photo.
You look great, Maureen!
So do you!
Geoff will be there, right?
Who cares?! He totally looks like a turtle.

Amber's been squad leader for a month. She's already made Richard do sixty push-ups.

My sister asked me to help organize Showcase Days...

But I declined. I joined Color Guard instead!

Here's a fun fact: All I had to do in Color Gaurd was hold a flag during school ceremonies. No fancy marching.

Another fun fact: Participation in Color Guard should give me enough points to get an A in Cadet Corps.

See. Still the thinker.

AGUARS
I was a lot less worried about the first big dance of the year once Bryce told me about it.

He's my seventh-grade buddy.

And yes, as others have said, he's very cute.

Hey, Maureen. Do you want to dance?
Maybe even boyfriend cute.

Maybe later? There's someone else I promised to dance with first.

You want to dance? To this song?

It's too fast and --

Are you nervous about dancing in public?

Maybe we could find a dark corner or --

Fran! Stop **thinking** so much!

AND JUST DANCE!

ACKNOWLEDGMENTS

Many thanks to:

My agent, Sara Crowe, and my editors, Cassandra Pelham Fulton and Nick Thomas, for helping to turn this prose writer into a graphic novelist.

David Saylor, Carmen Alvarez, Lizette Serrano, Emily Heddleson, Danielle Yadao, Elisabeth Ferrari, along with so many others at Scholastic, for your continued support of my career.

Shannon Wright, for bringing Maureen, Francine, and the crew to life in ways that exceeded expectations in every way possible.

Jenni Holm, Gene Yang, Shannon Hale, and Raina Telgemeier, for your guidance on graphic novel scripts and process.

My Beverly Shores crew, for your early feedback on this project.

My family, as always, for your everlasting support.

And finally — Brad and Andrea, and Savannah and Sydney — for gifting me with a lifetime of stories. While this novel isn't a memoir, the emotions — and the love — are real and true.

VARIAN

With my twin, Brad, and sister, Andrea.
We're nine and she's five.

Photo by Kenneth Gall

VARIAN JOHNSON is the author of nine novels, including *The Parker Inheritance*, which was a Coretta Scott King Honor Book and a Boston Globe–Horn Book Award Honor Book, and *The Great Greene Heist*, which was an ALA Notable Children's Book and a Kirkus Reviews Best Book of 2014. He received an MFA from Vermont College of Fine Arts, where he now serves as a member of the faculty. Varian lives outside of Austin, Texas, with his family. To learn more, visit him online at varianjohnson.com.

Photo by Sarah Schultz-Taylor

SHANNON WRIGHT is an illustrator and cartoonist based in Richmond, Virginia. She has illustrated two picture books, *My Mommy Medicine* by Edwidge Danticat and *I'm Gonna Push Through* by Jasmyn Wright. She also provided the cover art for *Betty Before X* by Ilyasah Shabazz and Renée Watson, and *Strange Birds: A Field Guide to Ruffling Feathers* by Celia C. Pérez. Shannon graduated with a BFA from Virginia Commonwealth University, where she co-teaches a comics course during the summer. To learn more, visit her online at shannon-wright.com.

Many thanks to:

My agent, Hannah Mann, for always keeping me grounded, and my editors Cassandra Pelham Fulton and Nick Thomas. I made my first graphic novel!

David Saylor, Carmen Alvarez, Lizette Serrano, Emily Nguyen, Phil Falco, Shivana Sookdeo, and all the folks at Scholastic for being in my corner.

Varian Johnson for trusting me with his story — our girls Maureen and Francine and this vast world of characters — and for truly collaborating with me. Thank you.

My friends, both physically present and online, for constantly looking over my work, and for providing feedback, mental support, and love during such a tedious process. You all mean the world to me.

To my colorists: Andrea Bell, Damali Beatty, and Lauren Pierre.

My flatters: Amara Sherm, Ameorry Luo, Dhurata Mehmetja, Jasmine Walls, Kyle Katterjohn, Laura Arce, Leila Arisa, and Sierra Wilson.

My whole family, specifically my mom and dad, for the constant support that has never wavered. Not now, not when I was a little girl, not ever.

Kelly Alder, who I consider my comics mentor (and my second Dad). You were the catalyst, along with Chris Kindred, for my interest and career in comics. I've been grateful for every critique and form of guidance.

And finally, to Brandon Robertson. I wish you could have seen my first graphic novel, the same one you always told me I was working too hard on. The same one you provided so many gummies for during work sessions at my place. And the same one that has remnants of you scattered throughout. I did it, Brando!

SHANNON

With my little brother, Kevin (but we call him Duke), and cousin, Devin. I'm four and they're three.